Filipino Friends

text by Liana Romulo   illustrations by Corazon Dandan-Albano

sorbetero
ice cream man

TUTTLE Publishing

Tokyo | Rutland, Vermont | Singapore

For Bianca and Katrina
and all junior ambassadors from the Philippines.

Looking out over a city that's new,
Sam feels lonely, strange, frightened, and blue.

Enero January

Pebrero February

Marso March

Tag-init Dry Season

langit sky

puno tree

bola ball

kubo hut

bangka boat

alon wave

timba pail

pala shovel

kastilyong buhangin sand castle

salbabida lifesaver

Abril April

Mayo May

Hunyo June

In the Philippines, the seasons are two instead of four.

Tag-ulan Wet Season

Hulyo July

Agosto August

Setyembre September

bahay house

payong umbrella

kapote raincoat

tubig water

botas boots

bangkang papel paper boat

Oktubre October

Nobyembre November

Disyembre December

They've got dry season and wet season.

Sam's family is very small.
There's only Sam, his mom, his dad . . . that's all.

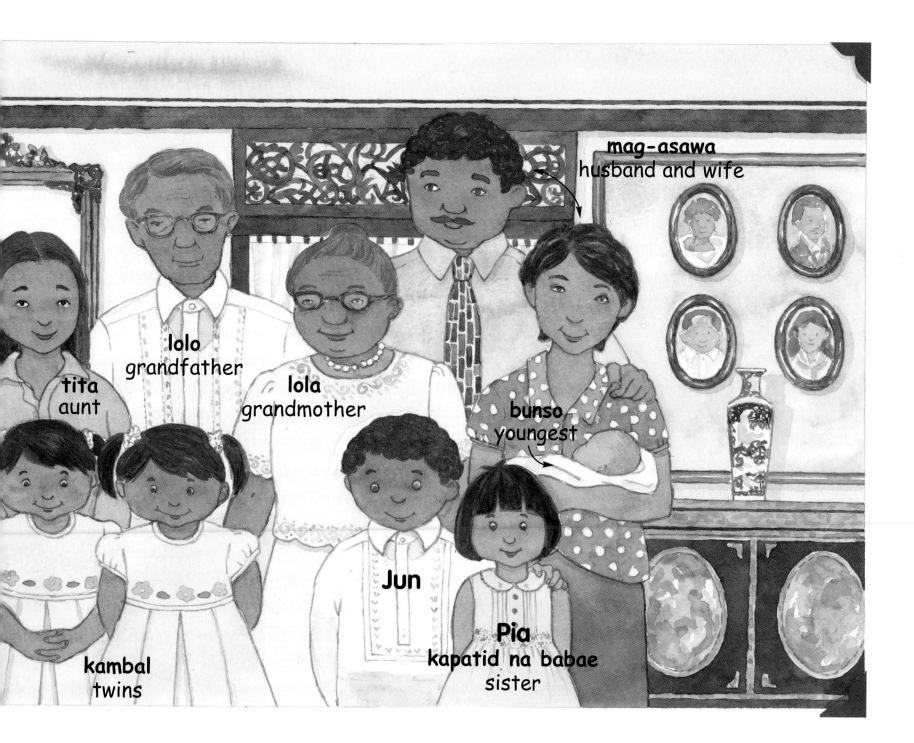

mag-asawa
husband and wife

tita
aunt

lolo
grandfather

lola
grandmother

bunso
youngest

kambal
twins

Jun

Pia
kapatid na babae
sister

Jun's is a family extended.
With cousins to play with he's always contented.

Sam shakes hands with people he meets.

pinto
door

larawan
painting

bintana
window

bangko
chair

Mano po!

Filipino kids must always show respect for grownups or anyone much older than they are. When Pia meets a lot of people at the same time, she knows she should greet the older ones in the group first. In the picture on the left, Pia kisses Sam's dad on the cheek. That's one way of saying hello in the Philippines. Another way to greet someone respectfully is by using a traditional gesture called *pagmamano*. In the picture above, Pia shows us the proper way to do this gesture. She bows slightly as she takes the hand of her grandmother. Then she gently touches the back of the hand to her forehead. Sometimes she even says the words, *"Mano po!"* when she does this.

Pia kisses as she greets.

palayan
rice paddy

palay
rice plant

palay
unhusked rice

bigas
uncooked rice

Almusal Breakfast

Sarap!
Yummy!

kutsilyo
knife

keso
cheese

gatas
milk

tinapay
bread

mantikilya
butter

palaman
filling

Sam likes bread with every meal,

Tanghalian Lunch

Gutom ako!
I'm hungry!

sinaing
cooked rice
(still in the pot)

kanin
cooked rice
(served in a dish)

ulam na gulay
vegetable dish

tinidor
fork

inumin
drink

kutsara
spoon

mangkok
bowl

pritong isda
fried fish

pinggan
plate

sinangag
fried rice

lugaw
rice porridge

but Pia thinks rice is a better deal.

suman
flavored sticky rice wrapped
in palm or banana leaves

kutsinta
brown rice cakes

puto
white rice cakes

prutas
fruit

Chocolate ice cream is Sam's favorite treat,

gulaman
gelatin

+

beans

+

saging
banana

+

kamote
sweet potato

+

sago

kinaskas na yelo
shaved ice

+

malabnaw na gatas
evaporated milk

+

asukal
sugar

langka
jackfruit

+

ube
purple yam

+

leche flan
caramel custard

=

halo-halo

but halo-halo is hard to beat.

simbahan
church

pari
priest

binyag
christening

lobo
balloon

ninong
godfather

sanggol
baby

barya
coins

A baby's christening can be kind of neat.

Handaan Party

ninang
godmother

bisita
guest

pagkain
food

bata
child

Philippine Coins

singko
five centavos

diyes
ten centavos

beinte-singko
twenty-five
centavos

piso
one peso

Sam's favorite part of the christening party was when the baby's godmother and godfather threw handfuls of coins up in the air. Following Jun, Sam scrambled to collect as many coins as he could. In many places in the Philippines, coin-tossing happens at housewarmings and to celebrate the opening of new offices; but it is a tradition that also happens at christenings and even weddings.

One just mustn't overeat!

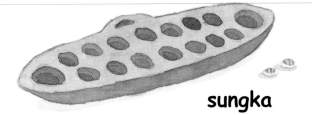

sungka

Two people can play this popular board game at one time. The board is made out of carved wood with two big holes on the ends and seven smaller ones on each player's side. When it is your turn, you pick up a handful of little shells and distribute them among the holes, making a pleasant clicking sound.

tira
turn

paka
shells

taguan

Taguan is exactly like hide-and-seek, and is just as popular. The *taya* ("it") counts to ten while everyone else finds a good hiding place. If the *taya* finds you first, you become the new *taya*.

taya
"it"

magtago
to hide

With new friends, cousins, and classmates,

panalo
winner

talo
loser

dama

Dama is similar to checkers. You must capture your opponent's pieces, called *pitsa*, one by one.

kalaban
opponent

kakampi
teammate

sipa

Sipa means "kick" in Filipino, but in the game it is the object that you kick that's called the *sipa*. There are many ways to play this game in the Philippines as well as in other Asian countries. Sometimes the game is played in teams, with each player kicking the *sipa* several times before passing it.

Sam plays games, like in the States.

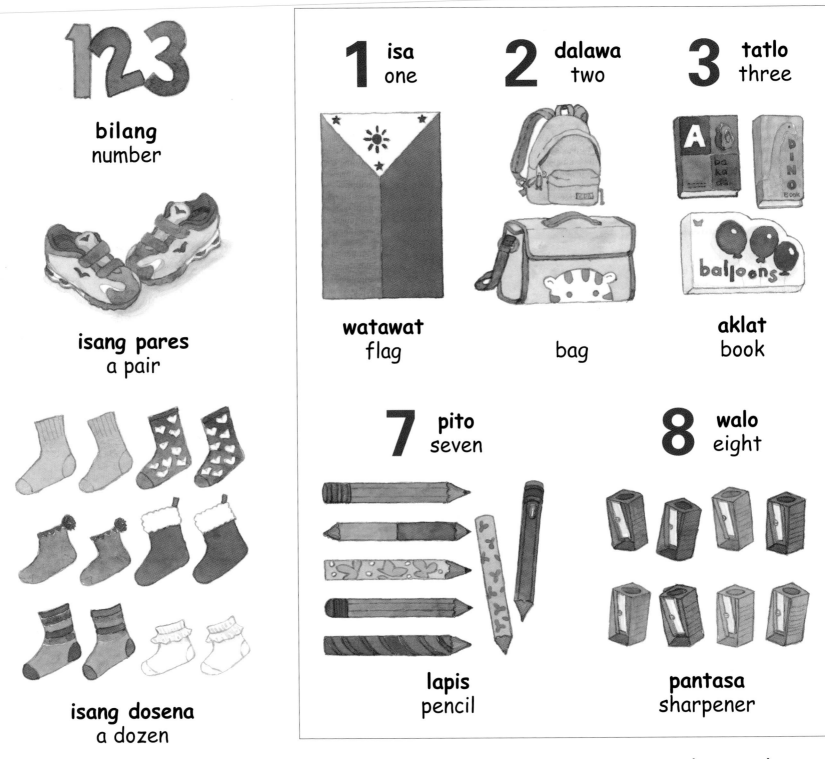

123
bilang
number

isang pares
a pair

isang dosena
a dozen

1 isa
one

watawat
flag

2 dalawa
two

bag

3 tatlo
three

aklat
book

7 pito
seven

lapis
pencil

8 walo
eight

pantasa
sharpener

Sam knows by heart numbers one through ten.

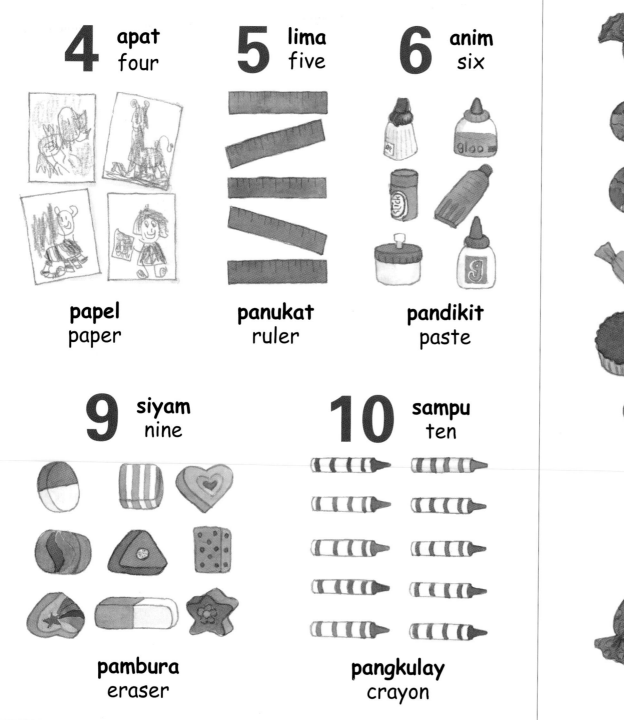

4 apat
four

papel
paper

5 lima
five

panukat
ruler

6 anim
six

pandikit
paste

9 siyam
nine

pambura
eraser

10 sampu
ten

pangkulay
crayon

marami
many

kaunti
few

But if he falters he tries again.

banana cue / kamote cue
bananas or sweet potatoes
fried on a stick

MERIENDA
Midafternoon Snack

mais con hielo
corn with crushed ice,
milk, and syrup

buko
young coconut

taho
soybean curds
with syrup

prutas
fruits

suman
sticky rice cooked in
coconut milk and wrapped
in palm or banana leaves

sorbetes
ice cream

nilagang mani
boiled peanuts

pritong lumpia
fried vegetable
spring roll

kutsinta / putong puti
brown / white rice cakes

sapin-sapin
layered rice cake

ensaimada
sweet buttery roll

arroz caldo
rice porridge with
chicken

fishballs

siopao
steamed pork bun

cassava cake

turon na saging
fried banana
spring roll

empanada
meat-filled pastry

sopas
soup

ice candy
frozen fruit juice

nilagang mais
boiled corn

kornik
toasted corn kernels

The kids share snacks late in the day,

hardin
garden

halaman
plants

aso
dog

Hapon Afternoon

either at home or in a café.

 The *kalamansi* lime is small and round, like a ball you might use to play jacks. It's green on the outside and yellow on the inside. It's sour and lemony, and it grows on small trees. You can make *kalamansi* juice into a refreshing drink. You can also mix it into other kinds of dishes, like fried noodles, to make them taste better, or squeeze some over other fruits. Other kinds of limes are similar but they are more sour and not as fragrant as *kalamansi*.

 A lemon is usually yellow in color and tastes sour. There are many different kinds of lemons, but the most common kind is about as large as your fist. Mixed with sugar, lemons can be made into drinks or even candy. Like the *kalamansi*, lemons grow on trees.

Pampalamig
Refreshment

halo
mix

piga
squeeze

asukal
sugar

yelo
ice

matamis
sweet

malamig
cold

buto
seed

Kalamansi juice tastes, oh, so sweet.

Kalamansi Juice (good for two)

 2 cups (500 ml) cold water

 6 to 8 *kalamansi*

 1 tablespoon sugar

 Lots of ice

1. Ask a grownup to help you slice each *kalamansi* in half.
2. Put a strainer on top of a tall glass.
3. Squeeze 3 or 4 *kalamansi* into the glass. (The strainer will catch the seeds.)
4. Move the strainer to another glass and squeeze 3 or 4 *kalamansi* into that one.
5. Pour cold water into each glass, about three-quarters full.
6. Stir half a tablespoon of sugar into each glass.
7. Add ice to both glasses.
8. Enjoy!

uhaw
thirsty

pitsel
pitcher

maasim
sour

baso
drinking
glass

Like lemonade, it beats the heat!

Philippine Wildlife

manaul Philippine eagle

The *manaul* is one of the world's largest birds and the national bird of the Philippines. It eats small animals, like snakes, lizards, flying lemurs, and sometimes even monkeys. Sadly, there are very few of these beautiful birds left in the Philippines, and they can't be found anywhere else.

pilandok mousedeer

As the world's smallest hoofed mammal, the *pilandok* is only about 15 inches (40 cm) tall at shoulder level. It comes from the island of Palawan, and has brown fur and a body that looks sort of like rabbit's.

mago tarsier

Tarsiers are only 4 to 6 inches (9 to 16 cm) long. They have big goggly eyes, huge ears, and dark-brown fur. They like to eat cockroaches, crickets, and sometimes birds and lizards too. They are born with their eyes open, and they live on the islands of Bohol, Samar, and Mindanao.

batige Maranao top

uyaw ancient jade ear pendant

Bulol Ifugao rice god

Chocolate Hills

These gently rolling brown hills look just like chocolate! For as far as you can see, these 1,268 hills are almost exactly alike. People travel from all over the world to see the Chocolate Hills, which are in the province of Bohol.

Museo
Museum

vinta
A *vinta* is an ancient boat from the southernmost part of the Philippines, Mindanao. What most people remember about the *vinta* is its beautiful, colorful sail.

At the museum, Sam had lots of fun.

kanungan
Manobo birdcage

Bagobo
basket

saklung
Ifugao dipper

Traditional Clothing

Apayao

In the province of Apayao, which is in the mountains of northern Philippines, women wear brightly colored clothes that wrap around their bodies.

Ifugao rice terraces

These are rice paddies built 2,000 years ago into the sides of the very tall Ifugao Mountains. From far away they look like giant stairs.

Mayon Volcano

The Mayon Volcano is the Philippines' most active volcano. It has erupted 47 times in the last 400 years. Located in the Bicol region, it is famous for its nearly perfect cone shape.

Maria Clara

The Maria Clara dress became popular among Filipina ladies during the Spanish era. Its blouse is loose and transparent, and is made out of pineapple fibers. A matching scarf, called a *pañuelo*, is heavily embroidered and is worn over the shoulders.

kalabaw carabao

Another way to say *kalabaw* in English is "water buffalo." The *kalabaw* is a very important animal in the Philippines. These strong and tough animals help rice farmers plow their fields.

T'boli

In the southernmost part of the Philippines, women like to wear embroidered blouses and colorful sarongs along with necklaces, bracelets, and fancy hats. The T'boli people use vegetables to color their most important fabrics, which are carefully woven, blessed, and handed down from generation to generation.

How to Play

You can help Sam and Pia pick vegetables on the way home by playing this game with two, three, or four of your friends.

1 You will each need a token to help you keep track of how close you're getting to HOME. (Choose a token that will bring you the best luck. A small stone, a pendant, a coin, or a shell would work very well.)

2 You will also need a pair of dice.

3 The player who wants to go first should roll the dice and move his or her token by the number of spaces that appears on the dice. Then everyone else takes a turn.

4 You must follow instructions if you happen to land on a space that tells you to go back a few spaces or lose a turn.

5 The player who makes it home first wins!

bok choy

labanos
daikon radish

araw
sun
MOVE 5 SPACES

GO BACK 3 SPACES

uod
worm

upo
bottle gourd

GO BACK
TO START

usok
smoke

kalabasa
squash

patola
sponge
gourd

kundol
winter
melon

START HERE

singkamas
jicama

talong
eggplant

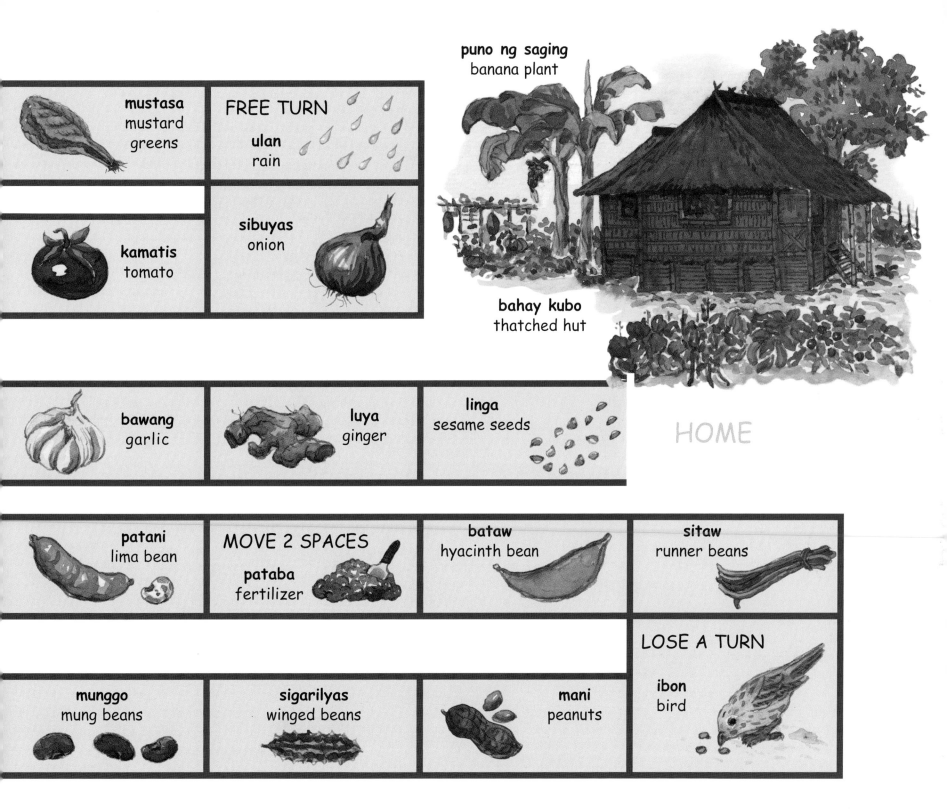

mustasa mustard greens	FREE TURN ulan rain		puno ng saging banana plant
kamatis tomato	sibuyas onion		
			bahay kubo thatched hut

| bawang garlic | luya ginger | linga sesame seeds | HOME |

patani lima bean	MOVE 2 SPACES pataba fertilizer	bataw hyacinth bean	sitaw runner beans
			LOSE A TURN
munggo mung beans	sigarilyas winged beans	mani peanuts	ibon bird

But the farm was even better in comparison.

Bahay Kubo Nipa Hut

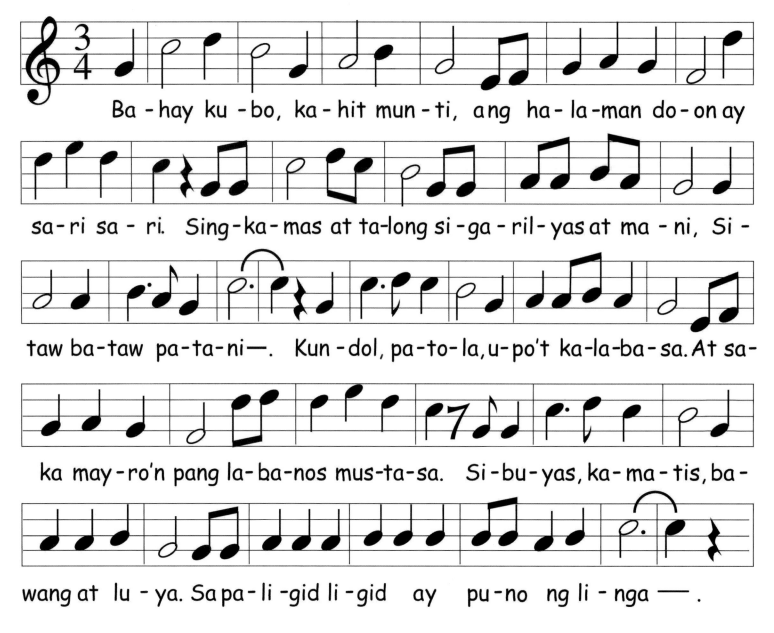

Ba-hay ku-bo, ka-hit mun-ti, ang ha-la-man do-on ay

sa-ri sa-ri. Sing-ka-mas at ta-long si-ga-ril-yas at ma-ni, Si-

taw ba-taw pa-ta-ni—. Kun-dol, pa-to-la, u-po't ka-la-ba-sa. At sa-

ka may-ro'n pang la-ba-nos mus-ta-sa. Si-bu-yas, ka-ma-tis, ba-

wang at lu-ya. Sa pa-li-gid li-gid ay pu-no ng li-nga—.

Filipinos love music, everyone knows.
Sam learned a song, and here's how it goes.

Bahay Kubo is a popular folk song. Here's what it means.

Nipa hut, although small, the plants there are fresh.
Jicama and eggplants, winged beans and peanuts,
runner beans, hyacinth beans, lima beans.

Winter melon, sponge gourd, bottle gourd, and squash.
And then there are also radishes and mustard.

Onions, tomatoes, garlic, and ginger.
And all around this are sesame seeds everywhere.

kulintang
The Muslims in Mindanao use the *kulintang* to make music.
This instrument has eight little gongs of different tones,
set in a colorful wooden frame.

hampas palayok

All sorts of festivals are celebrated throughout the Philippines all year round. Very often there are games for everyone. *Hampas palayok* means "strike the clay pot" in Filipino. The blindfolded person swings a bat and tries to strike a clay pot filled with candies. Once he or she breaks the pot, everyone is free to gather up as many candies as they can.

pansit
noodles

bilao
bamboo tray

biko
sweetened
rice cakes

palayok
clay pot

mansanas
apple

bagoong
shrimp paste

kare-kare
stew of oxtail,
vegetables, and
peanuts

dahon ng saging
banana leaf

alimango
crabs

sariwang lumpia
fresh vegetable
spring rolls

Of fiestas, too, sometimes singing is part,

Pista Feast or Festival

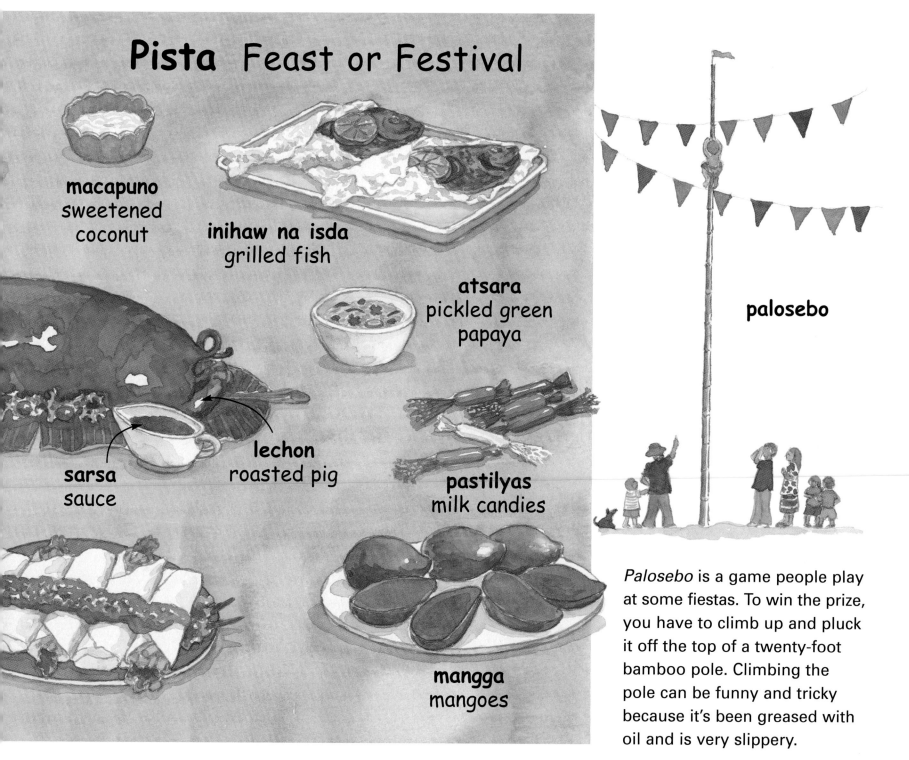

macapuno
sweetened
coconut

inihaw na isda
grilled fish

atsara
pickled green
papaya

sarsa
sauce

lechon
roasted pig

pastilyas
milk candies

mangga
mangoes

palosebo

Palosebo is a game people play at some fiestas. To win the prize, you have to climb up and pluck it off the top of a twenty-foot bamboo pole. Climbing the pole can be funny and tricky because it's been greased with oil and is very slippery.

while games uplift even the heaviest heart.

29

belen
A scene about the birth of Jesus.

fruitcake

misa de gallo
Misa de gallo means "rooster's mass" in Spanish. It is called this because roosters crow very early in the morning, and these special thanksgiving masses take place at 4 a.m., for nine days, just before Christmas.

parol
Christmas star lantern

Pasko
Christmas

The weather is warm, though it is December.

nyebe
snow

gwantes
gloves

**puto bumbong
at bibingka**
Special rice cakes that
Filipinos enjoy especially
around Christmas.

noche buena
Noche buena means "good
night" in Spanish. After
hearing a midnight mass
on the eve of Christmas,
Filipinos celebrate with
relatives. Eating, drinking,
and gift-giving go on
until the wee hours of the
next morning.

regalo
present

Mittens and snowmen Sam can only remember.

At the end of the day, Sam's content to stay
in a tropical new home with many beaches to roam.

A *balikbayan* Sam's happy to be—
a Filipino returned to his country!